If You Give a Deer a Carrot

by Paul Pineapple
illustrations by Balarupa Studio

...later she will bring a friend.

And if you feed her friend a carrot,
he'll tell his Mom, and Mom will send...

...all his uncles, aunts, and cousins!
Hooves will knock upon your door.

Deer will charge in through your window.
Deer will scratch your kitchen floor.

Deer will chew up all your curtains.
Deer will chase after your car.

And when they catch it, you will realize
This whole deer thing's gone too far.

BUT...

...deny those deer the carrots
That they've all come to expect...

...They'll go and eat your neighbor's garden,
Get your neighbors all upset.

"Why did all these deer come out?
We rarely see but one or two.
Did someone feed a deer a carrot?
Kid next door, was it you?"

What will you say? Will you admit
That what your neighbors think is true?

"I never fed a deer a carrot!
Why do you get all the fun?
I'll take a whole bag out. You dared it!
You won't be the only one."

The deer will gather round your sis
Till you can't even see her head.
They'll see her five-pound bag of carrots.
They'll do her bidding to be fed.

They'll pick her up and let her ride them,
Take her off into the woods.

They'll kneel down and let her knight them.
She'll become their queen of food.

But when the bag runs out, they'll leave.
You'll find her sitting in the mud,
Rubbing her face, crying her eyes out.
"Deer just want carrots! Deer can't love!"

You'll bring your sister home for dinner,
And your Mom will not be pleased.
"Why's she so dirty? Why's she crying?
And is that a cut? It bleeds."

Meanwhile your Dad will crack the fridge
And see his dinner plans are waste.
"I planned a nice carrot soufflé?
But there's no carrots! Kids: eat paste!"

You'll go to bed with tummies gurgling,
Hope to sleep, but know you won't.
So never feed a deer a carrot.

Just don't.

Did you like this book?
Leave a review on Amazon!

Want another Paul Pineapple book?
Read *Kooky Rooster Finds an Egg Sitter*.

Made in the USA
Middletown, DE
05 March 2021